**FOR CHARLIE**

Text copyright © 2006 by Harriet Ziefert
Illustrations copyright © 2006 by Emily Bolam
All rights reserved / CIP Data is available.
Published in the United States 2006 by
🍎 Blue Apple Books
515 Valley Street, Maplewood, N.J. 07040
www.blueapplebooks.com
Distributed in the U.S. by Chronicle Books
First Edition
Printed in China

ISBN 13: 978-1-59354-141-5
ISBN 10: 1-59354-141-4

1  3  5  7  9  10  8  6  4  2

# BUZZY'S BIG BEACH BOOK

## HARRIET ZIEFERT • EMILY BOLAM

Blue Apple Books

Buzzy is busy in the sand.

He builds a castle. It's quite grand.

Daddy asks Buzzy,
"Are you all done?"

"No," says Buzzy,
"I'm having fun!"

# Daddy sees a big wave come.

Daddy says, "We'd better run!"

Buzzy's castle is washed away.

Buzzy no longer
wants to play!

Daddy says, "Buzzy,
I know you feel bad.

Let's build together,
so you won't be sad."

Daddy and Buzzy get busy once more.
They build a castle bigger than before.

"If this castle is washed away,
I'll build another on a different day."

# PART TWO
# BRAVE BUZZY

Daddy says, "Okay, Buzzy.
Let's get wet."

But Buzzy isn't ready yet.

Time to go in and wet your feet.
Ocean swimming is really neat.

Fish that bite? No way!
Now it's time for water play.

Jellyfish? Not today.
It's REALLY time for water play!

Water too cold? No, it's not.
No one wants the ocean hot.

Daddy says, "Buzzy, here's what we'll do.
We'll go in together. I'll carry you!"

Buzzy says, "Okay! Okay!
I'll try swimming in the bay."

Buzzy says, "Daddy, this is really fun.
I like the water, waves, and sun."

Buzzy, Buzzy, is so brave.
Watch him jump into a gentle wave!

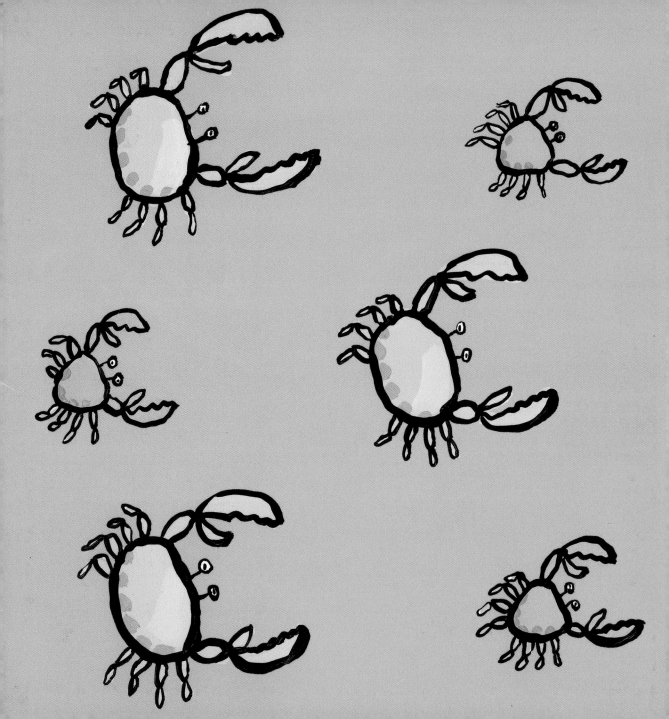